Sweet, Savory & Salty

Writing from Star Island

Written & Illustrated by
Liz Ames

DEAR JUDY,

WITH MUCH LOVE,

LIZ

For Anna
Zach
who love Star Island

INTRODUCTION

One of the most creative spots on earth for me is the Pink Parlor. This elegant Edwardian room graces the first floor of the Oceanic Hotel on Star Island, Isle of Shoals, off the rocky coast of New Hampshire. There, in late August, I sit elbow to elbow in a Writing Circle surrounded by the parlor's pink patterned wallpaper, as if inside a seashell. Some days we are 15 in number, and others up to 35, as we listen, write and then read our pieces aloud to the Circle attendees. Each morning from 2004 to 2019, our teacher extraordinaire Ellen Schmidt has led this workshop during the Life on A Star II (LOAS II) summer arts conference on Star.

From 10:30 am to noon, I gaze out as I write from my perch on one of the turn-of-the-century autumnal colored couches, watching the Atlantic through lacy white curtains, as the waters alternate a blue-green and green-grey. Over 15 years, looking out on this oceanic perspective, I have written about 100 pieces, mostly fiction.

That parlor offers up an alchemy. It is one mixed with 100+ years of history as a Unitarian-Universalist arts retreat and conference center, plus a cultural legacy left behind from the summer salons hosted by poet Celia Thaxter and attended by literary, artistic and other 19th century icons, including Harriet Beecher Stowe, Childe Hassam, Nathaniel Hawthorne and Oliver Wendell Holmes.

Through many dreary winters, Star Island has been my North Star. All year, I long for late August when the conference takes place. My elation starts as I pull the car up to Isles of Shoals Steamship Company in Portsmouth, New Hampshire, where my two kids, Anna and Zach, my mother, Lois Ames, and I will step aboard the Thomas Laighton ferry to Star. For one week our best selves will shine through. In my writing workshop, I will smile, laugh and even chortle because of the exhilaration I experience as I write. The Pink Parlor is the place where I have constant creative jubilation. It's as if I am riding bareback at a gallop, thrilled to the bone, or standing in bright white overalls, paintbrush in hand, surveying paint pots that brim with colors: yellow, orange, red, blue, green. It's no wonder Ellen has commented on the painterly quality of my writing.

On Star, I can let the busyness of life fall away, knowing that Zachary and Anna are happily involved in his and her kids' or teens' programs and that my mother has headed to her own creative class. The files on my law desk that pile up during the week of LOAS II fade away, the emails from anxious immigration clients go unanswered, and U.S. Citizenship and Immigration Service (USCIS) requests for further evidence are put off another week. Instead, I breathe, close my eyes, breathe some more, and open my eyes to Ellen's reminder that we can "write ourselves into any place we want." She then offers up a "spark" as an invitation to write. Some sparks have taken me back to a real time and others to fictional places through prompts such as: a hand, large or small; a piece of clothing, mine or another's; or a small red rectangular ticket marked ADMIT ONE.

For a few minutes as the group writes, it is silent except for the scratching of pens, distant porch voices and far-off cries of sea gulls as we scrawl in our notebooks, stop to reflect, cross out, draw a continuation arrow, tumble a sentence out, and another, and another—and dash to conclude the piece. Each summer, I have dipped into my writing pot and pulled out characters and scenes I had never conjured up before: a red-haired woman with tresses that cover a street; a koala bear that tells salty jokes; a sweet shop owner who sells magical, green-colored candies; and a piece about growing my new ears.

Over the years, my writing has also borne witness to great sadness and life's tumults: the death of my 50-year-old husband, Jeff Russian, and the raising of a five-year-old son alone, but also the joy of adopting my daughter from Armenia, to falling in and out of love, to selling our Central Park West apartment and moving to Harlem. One year, my writing friends and I filled the Pink Parlor with grief as three of us in a row read aloud our painful, poignant pieces composed on what I came to call "The Weepy Couch."

Each year in Ellen's class, I marvel that a word, a phrase or an image conjures up an entire universe for the workshop members. These beautifully crafted pieces have included an ode to a martini, an homage to a mother through her living spaces, a humorous story about hair products that makes the room laugh and a Billboard-like hit written by a musician in 10 minutes. As we reluctantly put our pens down to focus on reading the raw pieces aloud, Ellen reminds us that we are giving a gift to the group by sharing our work. We respond to the reader using her four helpful guidelines of being kind, encouraging, honest and specific. Not surprisingly, the majority opt to read their freshly created piece to the group.

There is a precious and articulated understanding that what each writer shares in the Pink Parlor is to be treated with respect and discretion when we leave the room. This knowledge has empowered me to follow quirky storylines that led me to create sweet—and savory—characters, which have, in turn, given rise to salty scenes. This (self-published) book contains 40 curated pieces from the original 100, lovingly compiled into *Sweet, Savory & Salty: Writing from Star Island.* I composed most of these pieces in 5–15 minutes in that cozy seashell of the Pink Parlor. The drawings were completed in about the same time frame (this year) except for the book's cover, which was drawn during my first LOAS II conference in 2004. The drawing by my late father, Bob Ames, is included in my piece "Admit One." I had wished he would one day grace a book of mine with his stellar drawings. Fortuitously, after his death, I was able to find a ticket sketch among his artwork that happened to match one of my pieces.

It is with great joy that I publish these pieces and simultaneously offer the wish that when this pandemic ends and we can reunite on Star Island, others will find this book for sale in the Star Island bookstore. This is a fantasy I've had for a decade and one some Writing Circle friends have championed for years. As you can see, this small volume marks several large milestones for me, including my 60th birthday this year.

So, dear reader, as a gift from me to you, I serve up these sweet, savory & salty writings, which I hope will delight and inspire you—to pick up that dried out paintbrush, to screw up your courage and saddle a horse or maybe to run into a sweet shop in search of magic. Enjoy!

Liz Ames
December 2020

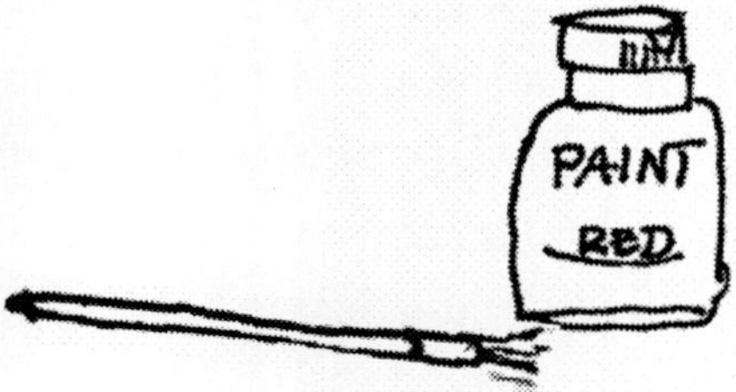

TABLE OF CONTENTS

RED AND OTHER COLORS

Red

They used to call me “Red” as a kid. On the softball fields, out on the playground and once in Sienna, Italy, “Rossa!” It sounds better in Italian.

I wanted to get my revenge. Make them see red. Big. Bold. Unending. I grew my hair.

A cascade. A red Niagara Falls. A rust and golden sun. An orange tabby cat colored rainbow.

It grew and grew. I used it.

I rented it out for red carpet events—sprawling, sprouting, feet-long. The tuxedoed, ball-gowned crowd marveled at the colors, the textures.

Beekeepers sought me out so they could weave hives with my locks, redorangeyellowgold fragranced with honeyed-lavender. Ah, and to wash my hair, the neighbors closed down our street, bringing out the hoses as children squirted scented shampoo across my tresses and rinsed them with rosemary waters. Then, my daughter and friends twirled and swirled and picked up my eight-feet tresses and piled them up like a stream of marigolds in their red and orange brilliance and laid them out to dry in the streets.

Call me Red!

The Perfect Dress

I rifle through my dresses: Chinese silk, tatted Belgian lace, satin ballroom gowns, Twiggy mini dresses with a matching white plastic belt, a burlap sack with zippers, *haute couture*. I need a change. A new *persona*. A restart. I reach into my dress closet for a new me.

I carefully select the 60s fire engine red chiffon dress, a stunner that shows off my figure, and zip myself in, sucking in my gut. Suddenly, my bosom grows, my cleavage plunges. I *ooh* in the mirror and notice I sound like that soft purr of Marilyn Monroe. I am Marilyn. I ache for a martini and another one. I lust for sex. Then my thoughts turn dark and gloomy. I need antidepressants, a handful, a bottleful. Hastily, I unzip myself, letting Marilyn fall to the floor with a sigh.

I reach for a second dress: this time the green Italian *couture*. As I touch the fabric woven from Italian goat hair from a mountainous region, on 18th century looms, of course, and slip it on, I hanker for cigarettes, strong espresso. I put my hands on my hips, admiring my tailored and hemmed just-so-right-above-the-knee dress. I saunter. I feel elegance grow inside me. Who knew? I am Italian! I am cultured! I am transformed! A restart. The new me. The perfect dress.

The Night Bathtub

New York c. 1908

Ella lets tumble her heavy auburn-red waves of hair, jumbled, tangled with lint, thread and carpet fluff. Her tressed hair falls to her waist. She sighs. Her thin white fingers are bleeding. She wonders if her fingers will leap across ivory piano keys ever again. Ella faintly remembers Beethoven, Bach…ah, Puccini! It has been years since she has listened to an entire cantata. Or heard the propriety of polite parlor chatter over clinking teacups and felt the satisfaction of ladling heavy cream over ripe strawberries and eating them leisurely with a silver spoon.

The carpet mill was especially dreary today. Perhaps it is the new supervisor Caputo. His burly eyes watch all the women, not just for the usual infractions. She wants to wash those hairy, groping hands away. She sighs. And then smiles into the night.

It is 2, 3 or maybe 4 a.m., but it doesn't matter. No one will be knocking on the bathroom door tonight. It is her bathtub. She has scrubbed clean the zinc-chipped tub that now shines white. She has an ocean of warm water before her. Ella carefully unwraps the creamy soap that she has saved her pennies for. Never used. All hers. A mostly dry towel and an *entire* room, all to herself. No carpet weaving, no back pain, no bloody fingers.

As she steps in, she is Queen Sheba. Salome. Cleopatra stepping into a rose-scented tub with water ladled up from the Nile River. Her hair is lathered by two maids with eucalyptus-scented shampoo and rinsed with peppermint-warmed waters. A perfumed orange towel awaits her when she steps out clean. She puts her foot out upon a hand-woven carpet decorated like a long-ago English garden of delicate pink tea roses, grey-green boxwood and a thicket of bushes hiding little brown sparrows that fly out when she chances upon them.

Sweet Marzipan

The little girl reads the sign and then presses her nose against the cold Viennese window to better see the Linzer tortes in straight, straight lines like young soldiers optimistic to be fighting their first battle.

She presses her thin cheek to be closer and to better imagine tasting the chocolate twigs and candied crystalized oranges and pirouettes of pink swirls that cover the layered cakes *mit schlag*, reminding her of the ballet classes she used to have.

She wants to touch the marzipan angels, golden-winged, blue-eyed with bliss, rosy red cheeks sculpted with permanent smiles, unchanging against 1939's political winds. She reads the sign again.

Knowing it is forbidden for her to enter the bakery, she tries and tries to breathe in the sweet marzipan smells from behind the thick glass.

Red High Heels*

You remember those cramped apartments in the 1980s whose stairs reeked of old cabbage soup and Stalin-soured sewer systems? Too many families living in too small of a space.

You, an American tourist, enter the Moscow flat after walking through a dim, narrow hallway, heaving from walking up eight flights because the lift has been broken for three and a half months. You walk by the babushka stirring a suspicious-looking gruel in a fluorescent-lit kitchen, Formica chipped, floor tiles unstuck.

A wife talks earnestly to her bespectacled, thin husband in rapid-fire Russian.

You are half embarrassed as you glance into a half-open door. The dirty sheets on an unmade bed. An empty bottle of vodka on the floor. An unshaven man just sitting and staring at you. Sad. Dead sad.

You walk purposefully through the once spacious family flat, taking away yet more of their privacy. You stride through with your Italian leather shoes, real Levis, a soft cotton shirt. You intrude, reminding them of what they do not have. Your clothes are bold colors that don't run in the cold hand wash.

You enter the room with Marina to exchange her Eastern goods for Western money. You scan the chipped religious icons as old as Moscow. You note the drab furniture, one or two pieces, and glance out the window at more concrete blocks, cracked, aging, half-constructed, and sigh at the lack of color.

Then you see them, out of the corner of your eye, high up in the closet. Lined up side by side. A set of brilliantly red high heels. These she wears when humming forbidden songs, her radio tuned to a prohibited station, its volume turned way down. Defiant, she hopes they will not hear.

**This piece is dedicated to Alena J. Ort (1937–2001).*

Titian's Model

1 March 1809

Dear Red,

Yesterday at Le Louvre I saw your portrait. Those amber cascading locks tumbled to the ground, making puddles of autumnal sunshine around your feet. Your ten pinky-white toes peeked out from your shiny tresses.

A copper sunshine of Tuscan sunsets streaked the skies.

Your hair is spun gold from Rapunzel's ripe wheat husks tinted with summer cherry juice.

Love and love,

Your admirer, not so secret

P.S. I forgot to ask you—where did you get your red hair?

Finding a Girl: Do Not Open

The baby is wrapped and swaddled with colored rags: frayed, faded reds and greens and gold paisleys, all clean. Starched even. Ironed out flat and carefully arranged. The baby smiles amid the colors, almost hesitatingly.

The woman, with dark circles under her slanted brown eyes, walks by, gasps and kneels. She quickly looks over her shoulders. Left, right. Ahead, behind. Searching for the grey uniformed police of China, their bony knees jutting as they march en masse.

The woman, in her 40s, maybe late 40s, hesitates, marveling at all the consequences that would befall her and her husband if she just picks up this delicious child. A girl, of course. Six months old or so, she guesses.

She thinks of the charts of her menstrual cycle tacked up in the hallways of her building, each month more irregular than the last, constant failure for all to see. Some months not even appearing. She has eaten special mushrooms stewed in bitter broths for six years, gulping them down each morning. For eight years, trying, striving, in the missionary position, not in the missionary position, but not even a miscarriage.

All she does now is walk by a quiet courtyard, a changed route, to find her rainbow girl, wrapped like a birthday gift.

A Robin's Egg Is Blue

God decided to swap out the eggs that year, without regard for shape, size or genes. The blue robin eggs for green duck eggs. Tiny hummingbird eggs that cradle in the hand were swapped out for thick-shelled, heavy oval ostrich eggs. Long-necked white swans' for waddling fat brown chickens', elegant autumn-colored quails' for thin-shelled flamingo eggs, Canadian geese's for sparrows', turkeys' eggs for petite darting yellow canaries' eggs, speeding with DNA.

In a big black frying pan, God cracked the hundreds and hundreds of eggs open and let the yolks sizzle. The eggs had been laid by ostriches and hummingbirds, flamingoes and canaries, blue herons and seagulls—crimson red, smoky charcoal, sky blue, beige, dun, ochre, cream, hot chocolate brown. With all these colored shells discarded, the eggs sizzled and cooked into a unified color: a golden yellow scramble.

The Floury Apron

It is a Marimekko splash of color: orange, yellow, red of optimism; dusted with flour (white, whole wheat); scented with vanilla, almond and a touch of peppermint from Christmas cookies; oiled with butter; plastered with sunny yellow yolks that did not quite separate; sprinkled with crumbs of brown sugar and powdered with confectionary sugar; dabbed with baking powder, smooth soda and salt. In its pocket, all around the apron front, lie ground brown walnuts, crushed hazelnuts, broken pecans and rainbow sprinkles from cookie batches; glitter from an ambitious star-glazing cookie project; gold dust from an even more ambitious dinner-party lemon tarte that was planned to be the *pièce de résistance*; hardened rose and red frosting from the cupcakes for the classroom.

My apron is a simple piece of cloth, dotted, smeared and covered in the mundane, the ambitious—and all made with kitchen love.

A Sweet Shop

Penelope always wanted to have a sweet shop—a candy store as they say in the States. She opted to call it a "Sweet Shop," giving it a European flavor.

Inside, there are baskets of marshmallow-puffed biscuits that are gnarly with ginger swirls.

Chocolates to die for and stacked sixteen high: dark chocolate, Kenyan chocolate, red pepper, salt & pepper, scented cinnamon, blueberry blitzed.

The best is the penny candy from her childhood: golden butterscotch with a green mint surprise that explodes with a tang on one's tongue when it hits the middle.

Scalding red hots that sear the mouth of one's worst enemy.

Peppermint lozenges to brighten one's mouth for interviews—that always do the trick to cinch the job.

Vanilla-scented balls that her customers hold under their tongues and spread a warm glow which powers the sweet sucker to lift the person off the ground and hover a few inches for five minutes.

Orange gumballs with iridescent rainbows that they chew until bubbles form to block out rude, bombastic speakers.

Shiny green frog lollipops that late-running office workers lick over half-eaten breakfasts in their apartments and houses so they can leap over traffic jams and delayed trains to arrive on the dot, slightly green-faced but on time to the office or store.

Penelope stirs her sweet pots of runny caramels, licorice rivers and melted pink cotton candy and writes out her magical recipes with her long stick in the candy-scented air.

FLIGHTS OF FANCY

Excerpted from *A Guide to Walruses*

Before I kissed the walrus bull on the end of his black, bulbous nose, I wiped his whiskers gently, wondering if that would calm the walrus down. Then I reached into my red square pocketbook, gently, fingers trembling, and fingered the leaves of the handbook *All You Ever Wanted to Know About Walruses*—and prayed to the marine mammal gods for insight into the psychology of a 2,652-pound walrus bull imported from Denmark which has been held captive at a marine show on the coast of Virginia for too long—and wondered if I could find the instruction page on how to distract him. How much time does one have before a walrus charges?

A Roman Boy's Counting Lesson

A Roman boy counts the X dishes for Caesar's feast for C guests

I. One tusked wild boar, his belly split wide, with green and red grapes pouring out, ripe as summertime

II. Two black and white ostriches, pulled to Rome by bearded Magi on a dusty leather leash, then slain dead

III. Three pyramids of cold tangerines layered with mint leaves, scenting the air sweet

IV. Four swordfish, grey sea-green, each long, pointed nose set straight against a bed of coppered seaweed

V. Five combs of wild honey, as clustered as Christian catacombs, dripping sticky amber liquid onto eager children's fingers

VI. Six red-shined pomegranates, juice running thick as the slow Nile

VII. Seven sparrows, brown and yellow still lifes, feet tucked under, a red arrow in each downy breast

VIII. Eight plumed peacocks, still and stiff, their eyes set with sour cherries and tail feathers as iridescent as darkened opals

IX. Nine spiky artichokes, cooked in the Mediterranean Sea, with hearts hidden in thistle covers

X. Ten pitchers of sweet, thick grape juice pressed by a hundred slave feet

Count, my boy! Count for Rome!

How to Be a Snail

They've all asked me how to be a snail. For a snail informs the world, gives stir to the imagination. We snails play a critical role in the universe.

First and foremost, a true snail must find a shell, a house, a resting place. Do not underestimate us, for we are agents of activity, changing our living places frequently. One season we are living in an artist's studio, the next a cathedral—a spacious space with long-winding corridors. Then, we may change scenery to something contemporary, or perhaps, in a family mood, we search out a classic snail-six.

The second snail lesson: we move slowly. We don't let anyone hurry us along. Slither, glide, stretch out if we are up to it, but heavens, snails never try to hop, skip or lope. Those pacings are for snail-less folk who lack the languor and love for millimeters, centimeters or even inches.

Third, we head for verdant gardens that have black, clingy earth softened by dew or seashores of sweeping white sand that will massage a snaily belly and then adhere nicely to a spiral shell's interior.

The lesser seashells who never move, or those soaring seagulls who can't stay still, or that seaweed that clumps and tangles itself, only to float away, unfocused, undirected and unshelled—they do not understand. Ah, they ask me, "What does it take to be a snail?" For all these creatures are unschooled in those three key instructions, the criteria to be a great snail.

Adventurous snail that I am, I have long lived dangerously. I am just a small snail. A rather ordinary grey-shelled, unassuming garden variety. The kind of snail one takes for granted and hardly notices.

Mine has been a long life, and I decided it was time: Paris, here I come! Perhaps the most dangerous place on earth for snails as those French nationals lap us up, coat us in butter, grill, sizzle, stuff us, douse us with white wine and then cook us alive in lightly sauteed garlic. I shudder.

But daredevil that I am, I pulled myself into my spiral home, tucked my black rubbery bottom in, squishing down my middle-aged spread, and began to roll up and down and round and round and round over kilometers. It was a long and slow process, but I made it!

Here I am, slowly spiraling past the Eiffel Tower, gaining a little speed, up the Champs-Élysées and pausing at Le Louvre to gather my dizzying thoughts. I unfold my slimy pleats of skin to rest a moment. Then, I refold myself gently in and roll past the restaurants where they gorge themselves on my cousins, aunts, uncles, nieces and nephews. *Quelle horreur*! Down to the Seine, one step ahead of tourists' footsteps, I roll right in with a demure plop. I attach myself to a damp, watery nook in that river stream. Once again, an unassuming grey, rounded snail on another adventure. Still unscathed.

My Sandcastle

That summer when I am ten, I decide not to leave the beach with the other kids and adults. Instead, I move quietly to the left, farther away, and duck into my sand castle.

The eight kids and a dozen adults or so shake out their soggy blanket, fold up the rainbow umbrella, sweep sand off and pack up towels. The waves splash ashore, making that rhythmic gurgling noise.

I watch them from behind my sand fort, through windows I can hide behind because of the dark green seaweed shutters that blow in the salt-sprayed breeze. I gather my seashells around me to line my castle with oysters, clams and little yellow shells to make the floor shine bright and walls gleam. The hermit crabs scurry out as I sweep my castle floor with stiff sea grass. The shadows start falling in long slants across the sand as it grows colder.

They chatter, bump their tin pails and whine and fight over who will carry the beach ball, fix a broken flip flop… Their voices ring shrill and harsh against the sweet-sea sound of time running out.

I walk through my castle, touching the grainy walls, pushing a seashell back into place, and dip my toes into the warm water pools that have formed. I am a princess in my sandy fortress.

A Garden

She had been an avid gardener in her day, with a flower garden exploding with colors and filled with perennials, annuals and even fruit trees, turning up herbs galore and other treats from spring to fall. She'd fussed and weeded and got sunburnt and boasted about her brilliant red tomatoes and emerald zucchini and purple eggplant. Her summer bounty.

But the rheumatism crept in. Then a bout of cancer. Headaches. There was a dizzying number of doctors and charts and re-tests of the re-tests.

She could not garden as she used to. Her fertile plot sprouted weeds. She dug up a few plants, herbs, flowers, just a selection to take into her house.

She had a couch, tattered with holes in it, blue and red flowered embroidery on its heavy arms. She tenderly transplanted her favorite rosemary bush into the holes in the arms of the chair. The lilacs into the holey cushions in the couch. The rosebush on another arm. And a deadly nightshade with its purple flowers and red berries healthy and strong. Of all her plants that she watered with a drip, drip, drip, she took extra care that the nightshade never dried out, never withered. Her antidote to all the doctors. Her garden.

Extra Sets of Ears

I have always wanted a new pair of ears. That's in the plural, twice. An extra set, at least, and maybe even a half a dozen to mix and match.

My ears are petite, well-formed, with two little earring piercings on the left from a night out when I was 15. They'll do. They're fine, but I covet new ears: one pair the size and stature of Prince Charles' with helix arcs the size of a waterfall.

A second set to help me fly, aerodynamically brilliantly, so I can flip them with a twist of my wrist to lift me high and make me soar.

A third pair that's more well-grounded. These ears will glitter slightly. Not Woolworth second-rate stuff, but Tiffany-quality with lobes that each boast a four carat empire cut diamond. None of this half carat stuff. Black Tie Ears is what I call those.

I need a fourth set for musicals, as at 55 my hearing's a bit off, fading slightly with the ends of sentences. These ears will be Carnegie Hall quality in large rectangular structures, the eardrums fine-tuned, highly sensitive to catch all the lyrics, hear all those tones.

Ah, my new multipurpose ears.

21 Ways to Cook an Artichoke

"I know 21 ways to cook an artichoke," said the fat, red-faced man under a ten-gallon hat.

"Really?" I responded.

He slapped a vacant-looking pudgy child on the back and yelled, "Artichokes! God's gift! Boil 'em, steam 'em. Celery brings out their flavor. Slip it in, near the end." He rattled on about parboiling, blanching, coating them in breadcrumbs, broiling and roasting options.

The man's self-confidence in his recipes filled the Greyhound bus that was hot and uncomfortable. His cheeks bulged, taut and crimson, as he blew up a green balloon, snapping it first. "Whaddaya want? A dog? Chimpanzee? I can make any animal you want. Except zebras," he chuckled.

His twin boys of about 11 or 12 nodded. I really did not want a twisted balloon animal, but I knew I couldn't avoid him, his artichoke recipes or balloons. Crammed into his seat, he barked orders at his sons as if they were slow prep cooks on a busy restaurant's kitchen line.

"Miss, take a chimpanzee. My papa makes them good," whispered one of the doleful, flabby twins—the first statement he had made amid the cooking instructions balloon tricks.

I watched as the man, grinning furiously and sweating copiously under his hat, twisted, rolled and stretched green rubber on the headrest of the dingy seat cover and wondered why he wanted me to cook artichokes using his recipes.

A Treehouse in the Deep Dark Wood

Once I had a baby grey owl that cuddled under my chin and nestled in my adolescent breasts. She was as soft as ashes, drowsy all the day.

I had six bats that talked to me in Battish and flew around my head like fish from a school in a dark green sea.

One thin tomcat with a green olive eye that sparkled in the white moonlight.

One morose, flea-bitten dog named Macbeth that itched and scratched and looked for bones beneath the earth amid fish skeletons, yellow fingernails and rusty screws.

We all lived together, the nine creatures and I, in an old treehouse with one star above that lit up the deep dark wood.

Admit One

I hand the bored museum guard my ADMIT ONE ticket and keep my sunglasses on. The guard doesn't recognize me in my big 60s black sunglasses, the blond wig and cherry-chiffon scarf around my neck. It is the newest camouflage to keep me under the radar for my monthly museum inspection where I scrutinize the exhibits, quiz the guards on attendance numbers and peruse my new, scrumptious catalogue.

My museum. All for me. Narcissist extraordinaire. Me. Moi. My fascinating ancestry, babyhood, teen years, my 20s (those European years), 30s (the cascade of lovers, all of whom kept my love letters—which are now brilliantly framed in hues of reds: rose, pink and two in scarlet), the 40s in funeral black, then the 50s with the money pouring in—the cruises, string of nannies in the wake, dog walkers, accountants, therapists, psychiatrists, masseuses, contractors, architects. The dizzying rotation of all those professionals for me…and the children.

There isn't much of the exhibit focused on the children. Well, maybe next year?

Ticket illustrations by Liz Ames (top) and Bob Ames (middle)

A Koala Bear on My Shoulder

I have a koala bear that rides on my shoulder and whispers in my ear. Its whispers are not koala-talk, as you might think, but ribald jokes. Salty, long-involved pornographic stories of sailors and pirates, accountants and executives, bakers and bishops.

This fluffy grey-furred koala is innocent-looking, with those big, doleful eyes and a slight Australian twang as it makes the delivery of its jokes. Crowds gather and cover their children's ears—especially those under 12. The parents pretend to gasp with horror at the dirty talk but actually chortle to themselves, smirking at the crassness let loose on a sunny afternoon in a public square.

A Pocket

I reach into my pocket and discover a folded piece of paper.

One of those origami-like papers that kids make at camp, in free time or on a Snow Day from school. They have numbers, jokes. You know—they're folded into eighths with triangle flaps that kids put their sticky fingers into, and zip-zip, flip-flap, it's the number two, six or eleven that the kid folds back.

But my flaps have a raven-haired *fairy* and a gnarled-faced *troll* and a *giant* grinning with an ebony tooth and a big rock under his arm and a *mermaid* with a sea-blue tail and skeins of barnacled seaweed over her arms and bared breasts and a *witch* whose green eye has popped out so that she holds it in gnarled yellowed fingers with dirty fingernails and *bats* that cover the flaps with open screaming red mouths and spiked white teeth.

I open and shut the flaps, then open the last one in apprehension and delight, wondering what I will see. There *I* am: blue-eyed, pink-cheeked, freckles across the nose. Fewer wrinkles than I have now. No crow's feet. Eyeliner even, mascara dabbed on just right. I look down and wink at myself (although I can't even usually wink). "Shh..." I say to me. The flap flips shut, the creases disappear, and my origami goes back in my pocket.

LOVE LOST AND FOUND

Dear First Love,

Is it the ganache? The broken hazelnuts frozen into a dark stream? An entire box of See's chocolates? Ones bought at the movie counter? Or the better quality stuff smuggled into the theatre inside my pocketbook? The powder paste gooed with milk and stirred in a cocoa cup? A fondue pot with a hot chocolate lake to dip red, ripe strawberries?

I'll say it loud,
I'll say it clear,
I'll say it in French, "chocolat,"
My friend, my love, my dear.

Melted and ladled over fruit. Roasted beans that are ground into a delectable fine powder.

Pour it.
Drink it.
Gulp it.
Never sip it, please.

Dark, never milk. White won't do. Bittersweet is good too (and greedy children grimace at your taste), so you're mine, mine, mine.

Walnuted, almonded, crystalized ginger too.

Chocolate ice cream, chocolate milkshakes, chocolate egg creams—never strawberry, mint or honeydew.

A pure, dark, gorgeous flow of my love.

My love, my chocolate.

Button, Button

“Button, button… Who’s got the button?” Isabelle said as she churned the milk and churned the milk and churned again. The other 25 cows lowed and stamped their legs and moved their immense weight left to right, right to left.

Isabelle, 21, pink-cheeked, with plaited hair that ran down her back with feathery twirls of escaped auburn curls. She milked methodically, with conviction, in the old dark barn.

Isabelle thought of last night: of hay straws and Jameson’s breeches and her linen petticoat and buttons forever. Her dress seemed to have one hundred buttons. Owls flying across the barn’s beams, hooting at their embraces, screeching at their ecstasy. Can owls smell love? Sense lust? Will the barn swallows spill their secrets?

She held the teat tight as she remembered the footsteps, the voices, the searching. How they scrambled to sit upright, their milky skin and raspberry lips disconnecting. How Jameson combed his wheat-honey hair so fast, straw flying, and nonchalantly threw his suspenders over his shoulders with a big smile at her in the still summer darkness.

She started to button, button and button, counting the buttons on her dress, trying to steady her panic. 100…89…76…58…24…23…22…21…18…14…10…6… 3…2… Where was the last one? "Button, button?" Has my mother found the button?

In the Doghouse

"In the doghouse." I took my husband's trite phrase, uttered through his grey, clenched teeth, literally.

I moved out of our marital house into Daisy's doghouse. It was cramped, a doggy pillow in the corner covered with white hairs, old cans of dog food in a cluttered cupboard, the plastic water bowl with "DOG" on it in red lettering. A canine setup.

I rolled up my sleeves and scrubbed and swept—and decided to re-decorate. I hung new curtains, lacy white ones that billowed in the wind as the sunlight streaked through.

Next, I added a floor with a grand bedroom for myself: cathedral ceilings, three windows on *each* wall. (He had long insisted we pull down the shades lock-tight against daylight or nosy neighbors—who would have had no glimpses of our lovemaking to titillate them.)

And finally, a roof deck with nasturtiums cascading redorangeyellow where I lounged topless, baring my middle-aged breasts in bold optimism, watching the sunsets.

The First Tide

Alice liked to go down to the beach at dawn. It was not for inner peace, meditative purposes, yoga or contemplation. It was for men.

Men of all ages and colors. Beardless, Bluebeard-full, mustached. All tall—six feet! And smart. She had a morning choice as she, a woman in her mid-60s with greying hair, walked down the beach barefoot, admiring the men as they washed up on shore. They were red-lipped—not blue-lipped—and full of jokes, dressed to the nines, a bit soggy albeit. For her to select from and flirt with, hug, kiss and more. She would choose just one, and the merman would gently cover Alice and himself in copper green seaweed to create a private salty sanctuary.

When their lovemaking finished, these mermen would throw Alice kisses from frothing waves as they submerged, reluctantly, back to Merman Land.

These brawny, handsome, strapping mermen had simply responded to her lucky skipping stones last year and heard her wishes that were blown over the Atlantic on a grey, sleety February day for a man…a man at every new tide.

The King's Favorite

Night of nights.
Dream of dreams.
Will it be life, or harsh death?
Will I romp in a lacy, sheer nightgown, or will death come down like a thick eiderdown, suffocating and still?
Will my king roll away, or embrace me with his crown on his head?
Will he murmur into my earlobes that I've rinsed each day with lion's milk, so they smell of promises of nightly delights to make him remember me throughout the morning and into the late afternoon when he's out in the fields a-hawking, and during dinner as he savors his blood red wine as he feels himself pulse with life and manhood?

My two maids have rubbed my white breasts with dogwood for sweetness, purple thistles for bracing love-making (oh, did pain) and black olive skins to make us slide together easily in the royal bed. Oh, those sheets of Egyptian cotton spun from Cleopatra's old cotton fields! The heavy curtains of purple damson laced with gold to keep morning light out so the night goes on and on.

Oh, let the sweet lotions of beeswax, ruby-colored with hummingbirds' blood, and shampoo of sugared honeydew melons and cornsilk that is spun from a hundred cobs please my king, my squire, my life!

For if my pleasures are not young enough, sweet-tasting and savored by the king, I shall not live through the night!

Rub my old skin sweet, my maids! Make it young!

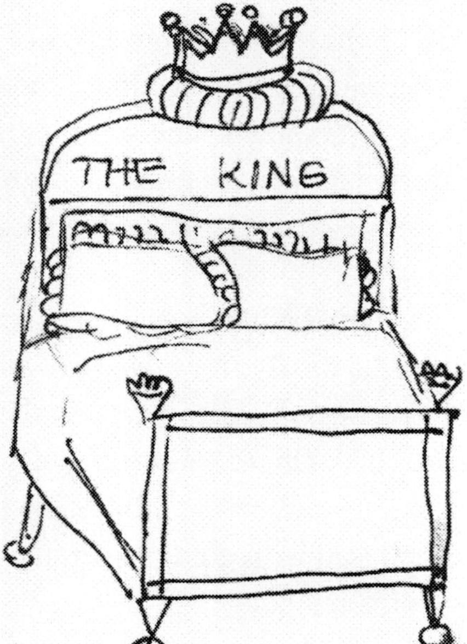

The Star Island Auction

–A quilt
–A two bedroom in NYC for a cozy weekend
–A romantic dinner for a couple
–A guided tour at a world-class museum

Linda had nothing that she could think to offer for the Star Island Scholarship Fund's annual auction. Then it struck her: her own gorgeous self, at 67 years old—not quite 70. All in good working order. And getting better. A treasure of sexual tricks. Better than a geisha. Rivaling a madame. A bevy of treats tucked into her lean, wrinkled body. She'd gathered quite a love chest in her day.

During social hour on Star Island, the auctioneer would laud her extraordinary abilities and make the men marvel—or women—or both. She'd write up a handbook of her romantic offerings: a night of delight. A beach day of middle-aged marvel. Out on the rocks on Star Island. At midnight in the chapel with lanterns aglow. She'd hum "This Little Light of Mine" in his or her ears all night long. The teenagers would lust over her and click their Venmos, bidding like mad.

Would they bid $1,000? $2,000? $5,000? She'd break records, bring in the dough. Hell, with her auction donation a family could have a *full* scholarship. Her Star Island volunteerism shining.

The Attic

Once a year, when the moon is full and spring is near, I open my cedar chest at the top of the creaking steps in the attic. With my long, cracked, blue-veined fingers that can barely rub a tutu's gossamer or tie a satin ballet knot, I close my eyes to see and smell the little girl of yore.

Her pink tutu is spun from carnival sugar, decorated with silver stars, gently cut from lacy cobwebs that hung across a kind king's bedchamber.

She has dancing shoes made of ruby red hummingbird feathers, laced with streaming velvet ribbons, covered with one…two…three…four…five lizard eyes that blink open at each pirouette.

She wears an orange honeycombed tiara spun from hard-set nectar wax from 10,000 honeybees that have gorged themselves on Spanish rose hips, French blue violets and yellow Grecian freesia.

Once, once, once upon a young girl's time.

The Wall

“Push me,” says the wall. “Gently… Brace yourself, my friend, for the dust, debris, usual plaster of paris. A molding or two. This is a 104-year-old building, so you might have to really put your shoulder into it.”

No one is in your apartment at 418 Central Park West, Apartment 105. You are alone in an old nightgown, a cup of tea in hand, perplexed.

“Go on, lady!” hisses the wall. “Don’t be shy!”

You, a 53-year middle-aged woman with a bruised heart, flip away the dangling ribbons on your nightgown, grit your teeth and hoot, “Heave ho!” Shoulder to plaster, elbow almost at a 90-degree angle, you push with your hip. Once, twice, thrice.

Your co-op board approved living room wall collapses, a domino effect that would leave a demo expert proud. You sputter from the dust in your eyes, nose and mouth, brush plaster bits from your hair and grin.

There it is: windowed (two, you count), Central Park views by god (which is not even true with your own apartment), 12′ x 12′ you reckon as you mentally start to fill the space. Your newfound room can house a mini art barn, a writing studio, a table to spread out all your ambitious projects. You picture the furniture: a voluptuous wicker chair, a long oak table that is honey-brown and gleams in the sunshine that laps the floor. You'll stack it with your writing journals, put out a jar of colored pencils—red, green, orange, yellow, blue—and a dozen pens.

"Like your new room, lady?" says the wall. "I thought it was you."

Le Métro

1984. Junior year abroad.

How I envy *les jeunes filles* on *le métro* in Paris sitting on their boyfriends' knees. Thin, lanky, smelling of fresh baguette yet weighing no more than 45 kilos. Chocolate eyes, thick brown tresses, high cut cheekbones. *Minces, belles, élègantes.* A black cashmere sweater thrown over her shoulders that never slips off, not even when *belle* she and *beau* he make out. For minutes. For hours.

I am single, red-headed, freckled, round-thighed. A standout in a Parisian crowd. Never blending in, especially when I speak French with my broad American vowels. And, I can't afford Parisian couture.

Those lucky, happy girls sit there: Gallic, adored, loved by their *copins*, kissing in *le métro*, embracing in full view. Is Paris the only city in the world where even public transportation is a place for love and lust?

I will return at 50, 26 years later, and sit on your lap. I will be weightless, balancing beautifully on your knees, never precariously, not even covering your lap.

And we will French kiss on *le métro*, not even opening our eyes as the stations fly past: *l'Odéon*, *le Louvre*, *les Halles*, *le Trocadéro*, *les Abbesses*. Stop after stop. The windows next to us will steam up, then the entire subway car. You will write our names on the window over and over with "*et*" between them.

A middle-aged couple entwined on a Paris *métro*. I will sit and sit on your lap, thin enough, loved a lot, envied by those young Parisian girls.

Lapless

"Can I sit in your lap, my sweet?" asks she.

"There's no lap left," says he, wisps of hair on his shoulders, fear in his eyes. She holds his hand instead.

She wants to crawl into his lap and sit as a queen on her throne, safe in the fortified castle of their marriage. Away they will be from Dr. P, the oncologist, who will not stop dripping IV poison into her husband, and Dr. N, well-meaning, gentle and kind, but always talking death in that euphemistic phrase, "palliative care."

She wants to crawl back inside his lap, into their own seashell of a world, where his deep-sea voice murmurs love words and the warm waters of his arms encircle her. There, her fears are stored away, bottle-tight, like medicines on the shelves of a bathroom cabinet. She longs for their old cocoon, evenly woven and tightly wrapped, promising a future and holding a past.

She wants to sit in his lap and talk of sparkling blue seas and sandy summer holidays and weekends in B&Bs tucked around green lawns in Connecticut. Maybe a weekend in Paris? All calendared, in bold print. Now, gone are languid summer days and voluptuous vacation weeks.

She wants,

She wants,

his lap back.

FAMILY TIES

A Pink, Pink Dress

A pink, pink dress for a six-year-old. My Grandpa Ames sent it to me for Christmas. Fabric as pink as cotton candy, dotted with puckered white balls, neat and evenly spaced. No drifting off the fabric like the sentences in Grandpa's letters that ran off the page at an angle.

My pink, pink dress also had a bold splash of red, right at the shoulder, where a long-stemmed carnation nestled onto my shoulder, held up by a green, green stem.

I loved to wear my dress to birthday parties where I would dress up inside and out: lacy white underwear which sometimes scratched my thigh and white ruffly ankle socks whose lace trimmings peeked over my black, Vaseline-shined Mary Jane shoes.

I marveled at my grandfather's ability to pick out a dress. I pictured him banging his white cane with its red stripe into the cosmetics counter, rattling the perfume bottles at the department store in Long Beach. I imagined him saying, in too-loud of a voice in that perfumed air, to one of those coiffed saleswomen with a beehive 60s do that he wanted to buy a beautiful dress for his granddaughter Elisabeth. The sales clerk would tell him in a patronizing tone to go to the third floor, stretching out the syllables as if he could not hear.

My grandfather would careen through that store, bumping into displays, walking into promotional goods, knocking into salespeople and other customers while searching for the dress of dresses.

He would hold out his thin wallet, containing his disability card and cash, and let the sales lady pick out the bills because his barnacled blue eyes could no longer sort ones, fives or tens. Then, I could see him as she held up the dress, tilting his head and squinting at just the right angle in that California sunshine, in that little pocket of light, for just a glimpse of that pink, pink dress with a brilliant red carnation.

That he had bought just for me.

M is for Mushrooming

I am sure she is there: a fairy hidden somewhere on the dark green moss. Dainty, ankles crossed, shimmery wings folded under her. She gently bats her eyelashes; they flutter like butterflies.

I am ten years old, bright red-haired with light brown, shimmering summer skin. I search for my fairy under dusty brown mushroom caps and behind unfurling green ferns.

I feel certain I will find a fairy, just one, in the quiet woods or along the stream where feathery watercress grows. Maybe up in a pine tree where she sits, sticky with sap. But can a fairy climb? Fly? Skip? Does she sip dewdrops with a straw? Drink from a brown leaf saucer and acorn cup? Or does she just sit, with a smile, in golden white gossamer on an acre of dark green moss that I have to tiptoe across so as not to scare her away while she waits and waits for me to find her in the still dark wood on a summer day?

Blueprints

I remember those blueprints that my father, the architect, brought home, rolled up under his arm, in the 1960s when we were small. Neat blue worlds of kitchens, bathrooms, living rooms, dining rooms, bedrooms with doors that swung open, windows to let in light.

My father, with his crewcut, horn-rimmed glasses, grey suits pressed with creases down the middle of his trousers. Tidy clean lines and delineations. Like our Chicago apartment where my mother, father, brother Adam and I lived. Square rooms, schedules, predictability.

On Saturdays, Adam and I would draw on the backs of those wide architectural blueprints. My father, the stellar draftsman, a protege of Mies Van der Rohe, would outline luscious, large fruit and sprawling vegetables with stems intact, and we would color them all afternoon: purple grapes, summer red tomatoes, black-speckled watermelon.

The coloring, the squares, the order and predictability ended with the divorce, which caused the lines to be rewritten, the shapes reconfigured and the blueprints not to come home at night anymore.

Tomato Sandwiches

Remember those new 1970s foods: Screaming Yellow Zonkers, salty Bugles, frozen popovers with runny raspberry jam inside, Hamburger Helper, the expansion of the Campbell Soup line and Chocolate Yodels?

Yet, for me, of all the foods a kid would covet circa 1972 was a tomato sandwich. The recipe went like this: two white Pepperidge Farm pieces of bread smeared with Hellman's mayonnaise filling all the pockets of the bread holes, slurpy beefsteak tomatoes as bright and red as a July sunset, an elbowful of salt, a dab of pepper. Close it up. Lock the flowing juices in. Cut quickly so the tomato slices do not slide out and slip away.

Take a bite. A second bite. And a third and fourth until it is devoured and there are the palest pink crumbs on the Mexican blue tin plates bought on your parents' honeymoon. Gobble down with Hood milk. Smile at my mother. For she was the essential ingredient.

Constructed, offered and served on the rare day she was off work and mother and daughter could slurp and smile together. No phone calls, no patients. Just my mother and me.

So Much Depends Upon*

So much depends upon how old the wiring is in an apartment. It's August, hot, muggy, Boston. Our ice cream truck has blown out the fuses in our turn-of-the-century Jamaica Plain apartment. We're in meltdown mode at midnight.

Robin and I, ice cream vendors at 17 and 18 years old, respectively, climb into our ice cream vehicle around 1 a.m. after repeated tries to bring the electricity back to the apartment. Ice cream trucks, the public would never guess, have to be recharged nightly, which involves throwing the extension cords to the roof, snaking them through the windows and plugging them in. Until all the fuses are blown.

Now, the chocolate eclairs are already mushy, creamsicles run orange-white, popsicles are sticky, syrupy, moving into pools of cherry red and banana yellow. I drive, fast, in a Boston night, hoping the freezer revs up, protecting our ice cream investment.

I marvel as I drive in the muggy night that by simply responding to an ad, completing a one-page form and showing a Massachusetts license, Icecream Adventures, Inc. rented me (the "old" one at 18) a truck filled with colors and love.

We, two high school graduates without colleges for September, head out into a summer night and are immediate stars whatever neighborhood we drive into: highbrow Cambridge, poor Roxbury, working-class South Boston, elegant Beacon Hill. Adults and children alike head for the ice cream truck even if our inventory is a jumble of half-melted popsicles, mushy chocolate eclairs and soggy cones wrapped in paper. All Robin has to do is ring a bell, and children point, trot and run in the direction of the jingle, pulling an adult's hand. Robin and I are the Pied Pipers of Jamaica Plain, driving at 2 a.m., averting meltdowns, staying an icy course.

**This is a line from a William Carlos Williams poem.*

Trapped

Trapped. I had him now: the squirmy seven-year-old with too many opinions in the backseat. Strapped in. His red booster seat lifting him up, just high enough so I could watch him, reflected in the Saab's rearview mirror.

A little boy with a nutmeg grating of freckles across his nose and a reservoir of emotions locked in under those chocolate eyes.

How would Zachary respond? What would my son say? I took a breath and realized that I had pictured this opportunity, watched the film, as large as a drive-in movie, a multitude of times before. Yet, I hadn't planned it out, sorted out the words, put them into a chronology.

We would arrive in 20 minutes at Grandpa's.

My heart thumped, the car bumped, and the words splashed out into the car's white interior as the Boston skyline appeared over Route 2.

"Zachary, you know how mummy likes children, right?" I looked into my silver rearview mirror and watched his eyes gaze out on traffic.

"I love you and will always have you as my first born and my best boy. Now you and I are going to embark on an adventure… We are going to adopt a little baby. A baby girl," I said.

"Where's she from?"

"Armenia."

"Will she speak English?"

"No, Armenian."

"How will she learn to speak?" He pictured her speaking exotic words, "gigantor" words as he would say.

Zachary's eyes pivoted forward, alert. He spoke directly to the mirror, "What will we feed her, Mum? Does she eat applesauce? How about if she doesn't like applesauce?"

"You and I will experiment and make her favorite foods," I said decisively. He paused, thinking of the baby eying Lucky Charms cereal in a supermarket.

"How about if she can't talk?" Zach asked.

"We'll teach her, Zach. You and I can practice with her every day."

Zach gazed out of the car window, thinking, weighing the information. "Mum, do you think I can have the 209-X4 Star Wars LEGO since you're getting a baby?"

You smiled. Success.

The Purse is the Mirror of the Soul*

My black-eyed beauty Anna, all of 15 months, can spend 30 minutes pulling out the contents of my blue and white big polka-dotted Marimekko purse.

First things first, her little hand reaches for the green glow of my Treo phone with its army of buttons covered with symbols. She grips it tight, brings the silver rectangle of the phone to her ear, waits, and smiles softly. Maybe she's hearing the sea, her rag doll, or is it me? Anna digs down, head into handbag, and emerges with my pink makeup case, which she unzips. A Maybelline mascara is tossed right, eyeliner tossed left, silver lipstick held in hand. Uncapped, capped, uncapped. A smudge of sunset red slips out. A mirror, more eyeshadow, a Chapstick, a barrette. Then for the wallet: American Express and Mastercard tossed in a whirring flash over her shoulders, dollars strewn on the floor, quarters, dimes galore.

I watch her pride and sense of achievement in removing each object. Is she seeking a specific item? Trying to empty the pocketbook? Accomplishing a task? Looking for the bottom?

For me, this cotton sack is utilitarian, bulging and overpacked with the contents of my life: a MetroCard, wallet, hairbrush, notebooks where I periodically write elaborate lists to organize my life. A pen or two. Smudged sunglasses. Jangly keys. Chocolate, if I'm lucky.

For Anna, it is a treasure trove to feel, to hold and admire, inside and out: a bristled brush, shiny silver coins, paper that is thinner than a graham cracker. What marvels to fold and hold! Such a bag of joy!

**This is a quote by Anna Quindlen.*

The Carnival

Seven-year-old Anna has decided to go live at the cotton candy carnival. She packs her overnight dalmatian dog suitcase containing her favorite ice cream pajamas and takes the grimy New York subway to Governors Island, an eight-minute ferry ride from Manhattan and 45-minute ride from her apartment on Central Park West. There, she lives with her mother, who never lets her eat sweets, and fabulous 14-year-old brother, who, when he isn't bouncing his basketball and will talk to her, is the bestest brother in the world.

Black pigtails securely fastened and sun hat thrown aside, Anna strides off the ferry's gangplank and marches toward the carnival.

There it is, wrapped in pink-spun clouds of cotton candy with its sugar sparkling in the summer sunlight. A cocoon of sweet, sticky syrup of liquid love, encased and wrapped with tight pink threads woven into yards of bliss, of dreams.

Rosy-cheeked and beaming, Anna turns the shiny pink handle of the softly outlined billowing door that wafts a welcome, and she steps inside into her pink, pink carnival.

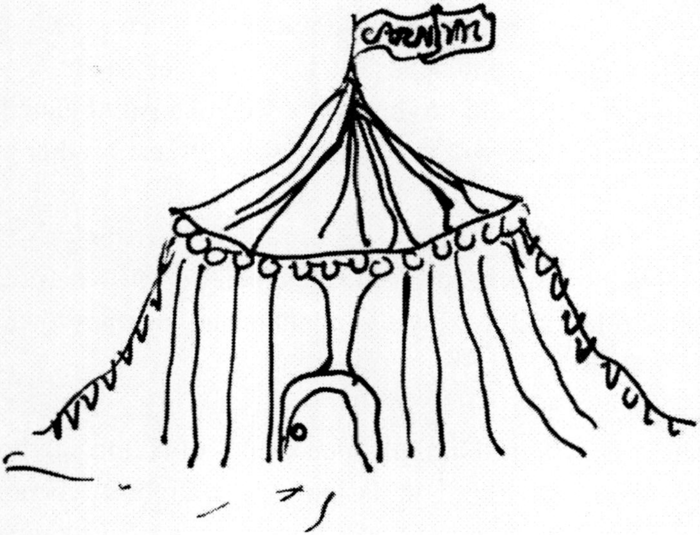

The Giggly Couch

I have left a sprinkle of candies on the couch: red cinnamon hearts, thick black licorice strips and two white Life Savers. Anna heads over and flops down with a signature pout, preparing to whine…but from the hallway I hear her start to giggle as only a ten-year-old girl can, uninterrupted, unflagging. It has worked! I have transformed our unravelling and faded blue couch into The Giggly Couch. When a discontented child needs to be redirected, I simply point them, lure them, cajole them to the living room couch.

I can toss out the parenting books: *1–2–3 to a Golden Child*, *No More Negotiating with Children*, *Parenting in Fear*.

Besides the couch, I have a chair that is emerald greenf with a bentwood seat. As Zachary, my 17-year-old, hurls invectives, complaints, injustices I've committed, I furrow my brow as if I am listening to his teenage litany and instead shepherd him over and plop him down on that other magic piece of furniture: a kitchen chair. Mid-sentence, he turns his cutting phrases on my parenting into compliments, expresses gratitude for my insights and pleasure in my company.

I am so very glad I rearranged the furniture.

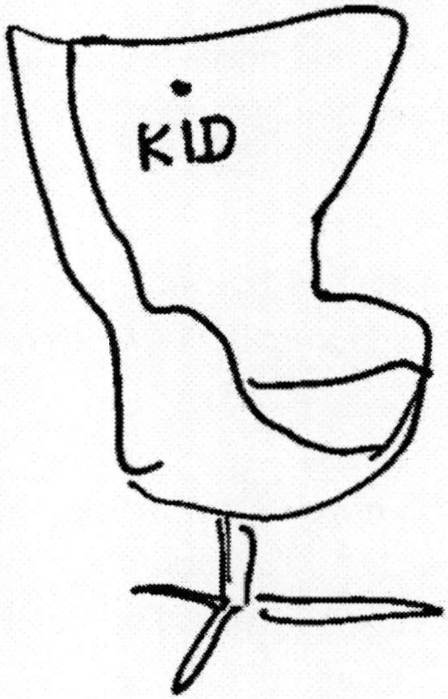

ACKNOWLEDGEMENTS

This collection of writing would not have been created, written up, rewritten, edited and curated into these four sections of *Sweet, Savory & Salty: Writing from Star Island* but for these dear, creative and supportive people:

Cindy Wollman, fellow Shoaler and years-long friend, has urged me to write—and publish. Her steady support has included many pep talks on Star's porch, a stream of check-ins during the year, and the gift of a notebook with "WRITE" on the cover. That gesture especially made me feel I *could* and *should* write, which helped me press on.

There is, of course, Ellen Schmidt, who carved out a space during COVID, a period in which she was teaching her writing classes and meeting submission deadlines for her second chapbook, and who, over 15 years, has been an unflagging friend, loving teacher and writing mentor. Her kind guidance, deft edits and frequent meetings made this book happen. She also gave me the first sparks to write the individual pieces, and then her gentle encouragement helped me string them together into a cohesive book. It came to life under her nurturing, gentle encouragement.

I also give multiple thanks to all the Writing Circle members with whom I've written together for so many years.

I must thank Rachel McVittie for typing and retyping and lending her calm, positive support throughout. But for her efficient edits, this book would never have been compiled.

There is also Marjorie Cahn, whose humor and wisdom have kept me looking ahead.

Further thanks go to Harvard Bookstore's Holly Youngblood, who offered strong enthusiasm for my wee book and its illustrations, which felt like an ocean of praise and drowned out my doubts.

My dear, dear kids, Anna and Zach, have cheered me on for years by allowing me space and time to write. Their pride and good cheer as I sought to complete this book fueled my confidence and filled me with joy.

My mother, Lois Ames, a writer herself, has long showed me the value of creating through the written word and taught me a deep love of books and language.

Finally, I thank all of you who are reading this book because without your curious eyes, attentive ears and page-turning fingers there would be no audience.